Fact Finders®

It's Back to School ... Way Back!

# School in the GREAT DEPRESSION

by Kerry A. Graves

CAPSTONE PRESS
a capstone imprint

Fact Finder Books are published by Capstone Press,
1710 Roe Crest Drive, North Mankato, Minnesota 56003.
www.mycapstone.com

**Library of Congress Cataloging-in-Publication Data**
Names: Graves, Kerry A., author.
Title: School in the Great Depression / by Kerry A. Graves.
Description: North Mankato, Minnesota: Capstone Press, 2017. |
Series: Fact finders. It's back to school ... way back! | Includes bibliographical
references and index. | Audience: Age 9–12. | Audience: Grades 4–6.
Identifiers: LCCN 2015048718 | ISBN 9781515720980 (library binding) |
ISBN 9781515721024 (paperback) | ISBN 9781515721062 (ebook pdf)
Subjects: LCSH: Education—United States—History—20th century—Juvenile literature. |
   Schools—United States—History—20th century—Juvenile literature. |
   Depressions—1929—United —--Juvenile literature. |
   United States—History—1933–1945—Juvenile literature.
Classification: LCC LA209 .G67 2017 | DDC 370.97309043—dc23
LC record available at http://lccn.loc.gov/2015048718

**Editorial Credits**
Editor: Nikki Potts
Designer: Kayla Rossow
Media Researcher: Jo Miller
Production Specialist: Kathy McColley

**Photo Credits**
Capstone Press: Gary Sundermeyer, 29; Corbis: Dick Whittington Studio, 17; Gamma-Keystone via
Getty Images/Keystone-France, 26; Getty Images: Bettmann, 7, 11, 15, Buyenlarge/Carol M. Highsmith,
27, The LIFE Images Collection/Ralph Morse, 28, The LIFE Picture Collection/FSA/Carl Mydans,
19, Time & Life Pictures/Margaret Bourke-White, 12; Newscom: Everett Collection, cover, 8, 21, 22,
25, Picture History, 9, UIG Universal Images/Underwood Archives, 5; Shutterstock: LoloStock, cover
(background); Design Elements: Shutterstock: Apostrophe, iulias Frank Rohde, marekuliasz, Undrey

Printed and bound in the USA.
009671F16

# TABLE OF CONTENTS

# Chapter 1

# FROM THE ROARING '20s TO THE GREAT DEPRESSION

During the 1920s the U.S. economy flourished. Many American businesses made large profits manufacturing automobiles and electrical appliances such as washing machines, refrigerators, and vacuum cleaners. Companies hired many workers to make these new products. With most Americans working, families could afford to buy homes, take trips, and go to the movies. People called these years the Roaring '20s.

The good times of the 1920s were the result of **investments** in the stock market. In the early 1900s business owners began investing money in stock market. About 1.5 million people spent their savings to buy stocks.

investment—money lent or given to a company in the hope of getting more money back

Workers assemble the first 16 millimeter camera at the Eastman Kodak Company in Rochester, New York.

# Buying Stocks

When a person buys stock in a company, they own a part of the company. Stocks are divided into portions, which are bought for a certain price. These portions are called shares. People who buy shares are called stockholders. When a company does well, the value of the stock goes up, and the shares are worth more. If a company does poorly, the value of the shares goes down.

Stockholders can make a profit by selling stocks when the value goes up. People often hire brokers to buy and sell stocks for them. The professionals work at stock exchanges, such as the New York Stock Exchange. Stockbrokers also give advice to people on which stocks to buy. Buying stocks is often risky. Investors sometimes lose money on stocks.

But by the late 1920s **economists** were warning people that the stock market was not stable. In mid-October 1929 stock prices began to drop. Investors began selling their stocks. By Tuesday, October 29, shareholders had sold 28 million shares of stock. The rapid sales activity caused the stock market to crash. That day became known as Black Tuesday.

Stockholders went from rich to poor overnight. Many people had to sell their stocks for much less than they had paid. And they could not afford to pay back the money they had initially borrowed. Investors could not pay back their loans to the banks. The banks went broke. Millions of people lost their entire savings.

**FACT**

The stock market crash also affected people all over the world. U.S. banks could not afford to invest in foreign businesses. People were not buying imported products, and companies could not sell goods to foreign countries.

economist—someone who studies the way money, goods, and services are used in a society

When people realized they had lost their savings, they tried to hang on to any assets they had left. They stopped buying new products. This caused many factories and stores to shorten employees' working hours. Unemployed people could not pay their bills. Many families sold their homes, cars, and other possessions just to buy enough food.

By 1932 almost 55,000 businesses had closed. By 1933 more than 9,000 banks had failed. In the United States one in four people was unemployed. This time of economic **crisis** was called the Great Depression.

Unemployed and hungry people wait in line in the streets of New York for food to be handed out.

crisis—a time of danger or difficulty

The U.S. government was not prepared to deal with the widespread poverty. President Herbert Hoover wanted people to work hard to solve their financial problems. He did not want citizens to become **dependent** on government aid.

Instead Hoover **loaned** money to large businesses. He believed that when the companies were again successful, owners could rehire workers at a good wage.

**dependent**—depending on or controlled by something or someone else

**loan**—money that is borrowed with a plan to pay it back

Many citizens blamed Hoover for not doing enough to help them out of **poverty**. People who lost their homes often lived in shacks made from cardboard and scrap metal. They called the neighborhoods "Hoovervilles." In the 1932 presidential election, citizens showed their dislike for Hoover. They elected Franklin D. Roosevelt as their new president instead.

During the Great Depression parents of large families often struggled to feed their children. Older children looked for work. Most could not find jobs. Some children dropped out of school to care for younger siblings while their parents worked or looked for jobs.

Hooverville town set up in Seattle, Washington

# Chapter 2

# SCHOOLS DURING THE GREAT DEPRESSION

In the early 1900s the type of school that students attended depended on where they lived. Children who lived in or near cities went to large public schools. In **rural** areas most children went to classes in a one-room schoolhouse.

During the first years of the Great Depression, city classrooms often were crowded. In order to save money, many school districts hired fewer teachers. Classrooms often did not have enough desks, books, or supplies for every student.

Many schools cut kindergarten classes and did not rehire school nurses. Instead, they saved money for supplies and building repairs.

*rural*—having to do with the countryside

midwestern rural school in the 1940s

Schools used money received from property taxes to buy books and supplies and to pay teachers' salaries. As people began to lose their jobs, though, they were unable to pay their property taxes. Public schools received less funding each year.

Some schools shortened their terms to save money. In some states, schools opened for only 60 days the entire year.

After the election in 1932, there were one million more students in school than there were in 1930.

School districts could not afford new books. Many young readers were forced to use damaged books that often had pages missing. Some classes were canceled if the books could not be replaced. School districts cut special classes such as home economics, physical education, and art. Teachers held classes for just the basic "three Rs"—reading, writing, and arithmetic.

Schools began requiring students to bring their own classroom supplies, paper, and pencils. Some parents could not afford the supplies. They had to stop sending their children to school.

Children often felt a lot of pressure to do well in school. Many parents looked to their children's education to help relieve them of their financial burdens. They hoped their children would get a good job after finishing school.

Advertisers often used the **parable** of the unraised hand to sell their products. In the advertisements for cereal, vitamins, or other products, a student who did not have the product was shown in a classroom. The students gathered around the child with their hands raised to answer the teacher's question. The one child who did not have the product sat slumped with both arms down. Advertisers hoped parents would buy the product to help their child be a better student.

 **FACT** By 1933 many public schools had closed because of low funding. This left about 3 million children in the United States without the opportunity to go to school.

*parable—a story that illustrates a moral or religious lesson*

# Chapter 3

# CITY SCHOOLS

Most children in cities attended public grammar schools. Students started grammar school at age 5 or 6. Teachers separated students into grades according to their age. Classrooms ranged from 30 to 50 students. In some large cities, junior high schools were built to prepare students for high school.

City schools were large brick buildings with many classrooms. Students sat at individual desks placed in rows. By the 1930s most public schools had electric lights, central heating, and running water for sinks.

In grammar school, children studied reading, writing, arithmetic, spelling, and geography. Students also took classes in art, music, and physical education. Teachers recorded students' grades twice each semester. Report cards were sent home to parents.

Children learned to read from the Elson Readers. The books taught reading through simple stories about a boy named Dick and girl named Jane. Class times increased as students went on to higher grades. Arithmetic lessons lasted 35 minutes in first grade. Lessons were three and a half hours long in the third and fourth grades.

A teacher assists a student in a classroom at Montefiore School in Chicago.

During the 1930s some teachers thought children should choose what subjects they wanted to learn. They were part of the **progressive** education movement. Progressive teachers spent little time lecturing from textbooks. Instead students often worked in small groups. They completed art and science projects and went on field trips. Progressive classrooms often were arranged in a casual way. Some teachers added window curtains, rugs, or stuffed chairs and sofas to their rooms. Progressive teachers wanted students to be excited about going to school. Many parents disliked progressive teaching methods. They wanted their children to spend school time on basic subjects. Parents often feared this teaching style would encourage children to not work as hard in class or at home.

progressive—in favor of improvement, progress, and reform, especially in political or social matters

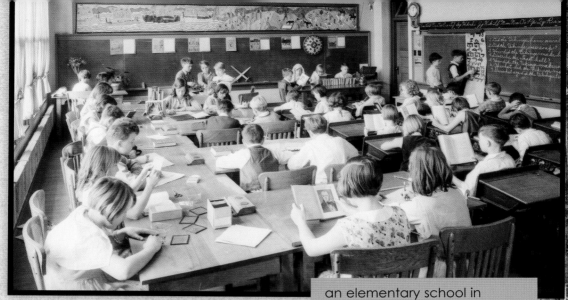

an elementary school in
Los Angeles, California, in 1931

# Teachers

School districts hired more female teachers during the Great Depression than they had in the past. School districts saved money by hiring women. Female teachers earned less money than male teachers.

During the early 1900s **urban** public school districts began requiring teachers to have normal school training. Normal schools were teacher colleges that offered training in classroom organization and teaching methods.

Most rural schoolteachers had only a high school diploma. The local school board interviewed teachers to test their knowledge. During interviews teachers answered questions about various subjects and teaching methods.

*urban*—having to do with a city

# Chapter 4

# DUST BOWL SCHOOLS

Children who lived in rural areas often attended one-room schoolhouses. Most of these schools did not have electricity or running water. A blackboard usually covered the front wall. The schoolhouses had wood or coal stoves for heat and lanterns for light. Students took drinks from an outdoor water pump.

Students in rural areas often lived far away from school. Children sometimes walked several miles to school. Some rural towns used a farm wagon for transporting students.

**FACT** Some districts paid their teachers in scrip. These paper slips listed an amount of money the school owed the teacher. Teachers took the scrip payments to local stores and exchanged them for food and other items.

Rural schools often had only one or two teachers. Students of all ages sat together in the classroom. Classes held between 20 to 60 students.

Rural schoolteachers taught all subjects through eighth grade. Teachers spent about five and a half to six hours a day instructing students. The students recited their homework to the teacher. When the teacher felt students understood the lesson, he or she assigned the next pages in the textbook.

A teacher and her students stand in front of Rock Creek school in Georgia.

Children who lived on farms did not attend school regularly. They often helped with spring planting and fall harvesting. During these busy times children attended school part time or took a break until the work was finished. Children often quit school after eighth grade and worked full time on the farm.

School districts around the country cut costs to keep their schools open. Teachers' salaries were one of the first cost-cutting measures. More than 7,000 teachers lost their jobs during the Great Depression. Some teachers worked for room and board with no additional pay. Some rural schoolteachers lived in the schoolhouse and cooked their meals on the wood-burning stove.

In 1930 and 1931 farm families on the Great Plains had **bumper** wheat crops. The large crops caused a **surplus**. Wheat prices dropped because people were buying less and warehouses were full. When farmers could not pay their bills, they lost their farms. People began moving west in search of work.

bumper—large
surplus—more than is needed

A dust storm sweeps through Rolla, Kansas, on May 6, 1935.

Between 1931 and 1936 the Great Plains experienced drought. The dry topsoil made farming difficult. A dust storm hit Kansas on April 14, 1935, which became known as "Black Sunday." High winds carried away large amounts of topsoil. This caused a large black cloud of dust to blow through Kansas. People began calling the southern plains region the "dust bowl."

Drought and dust storms forced many families to leave their farms. Families traveled west to California in search of work. They were called migrants. Migrant families often lived out of their cars or in tents. When money ran out, some sold their belongings, cars, and tents in order to buy food. After traveling many miles, some migrants discovered that jobs were scarce.

Migrants who came to California from Oklahoma were called Okies. Okies often were treated poorly for wearing old clothing and talking with a southern accent. Migrant children were behind in school lessons after months of traveling. Children placed in a grade based on their age were not ready for the harder lessons.

Migrant children were ashamed that they were poor. Some students walked home instead of taking a bus. They did not want their classmates to know that they lived in tents.

A father repairs a tire on the family vehicle as they travel in search of work.

Route 66
Great Plains region
dust bowl region

# Traveling Route 66

Farmers living in the dust bowl experienced hard times during the drought. Dust storms continued to hit the Great Plains for five years. Crops did not grow because there was not enough rainfall. Farmers lost money and they were unable to pay their bills. Many farm families left the Great Plains and moved west in search of work. They packed their belongings into their cars and strapped mattresses to the roof. They drove on Route 66 through Oklahoma. They crossed the Black Mountains and the Mojave Desert on their way into southern California. Cars sometimes broke down along the way or overheated in the desert. Families then grabbed what they could carry and began walking.

# Chapter 5

# NEW DEAL SCHOOLS

President Franklin D. Roosevelt created many programs to help people during the Great Depression. Families listened to his plans for economic **recovery** during radio talks called "fireside chats." He called his plans to end the Great Depression the "New Deal."

The New Deal established government agencies whose purpose was to create jobs for Americans. One agency was the Civilian Conservation Corps (CCC). The CCC hired people to plant trees, clear campgrounds, and build dams. Roosevelt also started the Civil Works Administration (CWA), the Public Works Administration (PWA), and the Works Progress Administration (WPA). The agencies hired people to build schools, hospitals, roads, bridges, and playgrounds.

**recovery**—a return to a normal state or condition

The WPA provided money to schools to hire teachers and pay for supplies. Through the WPA, first lady Eleanor Roosevelt set up a hot lunch program in schools. Public schools provided free hot lunches to more than 119,000 needy students daily.

The government provided money to build and repair thousands of schools. Workers added classrooms to rural schools. The New Deal programs reduced overcrowding in public schools. And government funding also began providing school bus transportation to students.

Hot meals included a hot dish, sandwiches, a piece of fruit or pudding, and milk.

# Dear Mrs. Roosevelt

Young people in the United States looked to Eleanor Roosevelt to solve their problems of poverty. Many children wrote her letters asking for money, clothing, and other necessities. Some children asked for shoes, dresses, or bikes so they could go to school. Other children asked for medical help. She could not write back to all of the children. But she tried to help them by creating federal youth programs.

Roosevelt wanted homeless children to stay in school. During the 1930s she urged Congress to establish the National Youth Administration (NYA). The NYA helped older students stay in school by offering them **grants** in exchange for work. Students worked in libraries and on farms in exchange for an education. Roosevelt also helped create nutrition programs and recreation programs in public schools.

First Lady Eleanor Roosevelt visits Vassar school in 1933 and distributes milk to the children.

The government also established federal camps for migrant workers. Families paid one dollar a week for a one-room cabin or a tent. If they did not have the money to pay for rent, they could work at the camp in exchange for housing.

Leo Hart opened a school for migrant children at Weedpatch Camp near Bakersfield, California, in 1940. Weedpatch School offered basic subjects as well as courses in various trades. Teachers held classes in plumbing, carpentry, and electrical wiring.

Weedpatch students studied agriculture and planted their own gardens. They grew crops such as potatoes, alfalfa, tomatoes, corn, carrots, and watermelons. Cooks used the food to prepare school lunches. Weedpatch School also had its own livestock pens. Students learned how to feed, raise, and butcher animals.

**grant**—a gift such as land or money given for a particular purpose

The New Deal helped many people find jobs.
But the Great Depression lasted through the 1930s.
In 1941 the United States entered World War II
(1939–1945) against Germany, Italy, and Japan.
Millions of men and women went back to work.
With people back at work, the economy recovered.
The United States' involvement in World War II
helped bring an end to the Great Depression.

New jobs included building planes and
ships and making weapons, ammunition,
uniforms, and other products for the war.

# MAKE TIN CAN STOMPERS

During the Great Depression families often could not afford to buy toys. Many children played with homemade toys, such as rag dolls, wooden toy soldiers, and tin can stompers.

## What You Need

2 empty coffee cans

bottle opener

thin rope or twine, about 16 feet long

## What You Do

**1.** Turn the cans upside down on a flat surface.

**2.** Use the pointed side of the bottle opener to punch two holes in the bottom of each can. Punch one hole about 2 inches from the edge of the can. Punch another hole directly across from the first hole on the other side of the bottom. The holes need to be big enough to fit the rope or twine through them.

**3.** Take the rope or twine and measure a length from your waist to the floor. Double this length and add about 6 inches. Cut the rope or twine. Cut a second length of rope or twine the same length. These will be the stomper handles.

**4.** Thread one end of the rope or twine into one of the holes in the bottom of the can. Repeat with the other end of the rope or twine and the other hole. Flip the can over and tie a knot with the two string ends. Then pull the rope until the knot is against the inside bottom of the can.

**5.** Repeat previous step with the second can.

**6.** Carefully place your feet between the rope loops and stand on the bottom of the cans. Pull up on the handles until the ropes are tight enough to steady yourself. Lift the ropes as you walk on your stompers.

# GLOSSARY

**bumper** (BUHM-pur)—large

**crisis** (KRYE-siss)—a time of danger or difficulty

**dependent** (di-PEN-duhnt)—depending on or controlled by something or someone else

**economist** (ee-KON-uh-mist)—someone who studies the way money, goods, and services are used in a society

**grant** (GRANT)—a gift such as land or money given for a particular purpose

**investment** (in-VEST-mint)—money lent or given to a company in the hope of getting more money back

**loan** (LOHN)—money that is borrowed with a plan to pay it back

**parable** (PAR-uh-buhl)—a story that illustrates a moral or religious lesson

**poverty** (PAW-vuhr-tee)—the state of being poor or without money

**progressive** (pruh-GRESS-iv)—in favor of improvement, progress, and reform, especially in political or social matters

**recovery** (ri-KUHV-ur-ee)—a return to a normal state or condition

**rural** (RUR-uhl)—having to do with the countryside

**surplus** (SUR-pluhss)—more than is needed

**urban** (UR-buhn)—having to do with a city

# READ MORE

**Fremon, David K.** *The Great Depression in United States History.* Berkeley Heights, N.J.: Enslow Publishers, 2014.

**Grant, R. G.** *Why Did the Great Depression Happen?* Moments in History. New York: Gareth Stevens Pub., 2011.

**Langston-George, Rebecca.** *A Primary Source History of The Dust Bowl.* North Mankato, Minn.: Capstone Press, 2015.

# INTERNET SITES

FactHound offers a safe, fun way to find Internet sites related to this book. All of the sites on FactHound have been researched by our staff.

Here's all you do:

Visit *www.facthound.com*

Type in this code: 9781515720980

 Check out projects, games and lots more at **www.capstonekids.com**

# CRITICAL THINKING USING THE COMMON CORE

1. Take a look at the map on page 23. Through which states does Route 66 pass? (Integration of Knowledge and Ideas)

2. The American economy did well in the 1920s. How did American businesses make a profit? (Key Ideas and Details)

3. What determined the type of school that children attended in the early 1900s? (Key Ideas and Details)

# INDEX